Aurealis and Ditmar Award nominee

CHARLIE NASH

Charlie Nash was born in England and holds degrees in mechanical and space engineering, medicine, and writing. Her fiction has been shortlisted for the Aurealis and Ditmar awards. She lives on the eastern seaboard of Australia, and is working on two new novels, and a third Ship's Doctor installment.

 charlienash.net
f authorcharlienash

Also by Charlie Nash:

All Your Dark Faces

CHARLIE NASH

FLYING
— NUN —
PUBLICATIONS

FLYING
NUN
PUBLICATIONS

Published in 2019 by Flying Nun Publications, http://flyingnunpublications.com/

"The Lady with the Lantern" first published 2015 in *Pseudopod* episode 428

"The Ghost of Hephaestus" first published 2014 in *Phantazein*, FableCroft Publishing

"Jack" first published 2013 in *Mysterical-E*, Fall/Winter issue

"The Edge" first published 2012 in *Scareship* #8

"Parvaz" first published 2013 in *Dreaming of Djinni*, Ticonderoga Publications

"The One You Feed" first published 2014 in *One Page: Brisbane* #1

"The 7:40 from Paraburdoo" first published 2015 in *The Never Never Land*, CSFG

In all the above first publications, stories originally credited to Charlotte Nash.

ISBN:
978-1-925775-13-6 (paperback)
978-1-925775-14-3 (eBook)

A catalogue record for this book is available from the National Library of Australia

NATIONAL
LIBRARY
OF AUSTRALIA

Cover design by Richard Priestley

Contents

For all those who know our dark faces and sometimes fail to check them, and who maybe enjoy that … just a little

THE LADY WITH THE LANTERN

The mine called Callum in his tenth year. One morning, he was walking to school with the other boys; a pair of new shoes, a boiled sweet in his cheek. The next, he found a pick in his soft hand, and his feet followed his father's to the cold, dark portal.

No one talked in the mine. Not in the gut-sinking lift, which clanked and shuddered as it delivered them, serried and sweating, into the earth. Not in the long drifts, where they trekked by torchbeam. Not in the side-by-side plots, where each man worked the diamond hard tunnel. Words were heavy and stuck to the rocks. They'd absorbed every story that had whispered from a miner's dark-crazed tongue. And so, as Callum turned off his lamp and felt for his plot with his fingertips, he learnt of the Lady with the Lantern.

She was an angel on some days, a deliverer who had rescued men from a roof fall. The rocks whispered of her golden light held high, making the broken backs of men into moons that turned their phases as she passed. On other days, she was feared, a ghoul who hid in her own shadow, lurked in the passage drifts, stealing boys from their futures. But no man whose story Callum absorbed from the rocks was one who had seen her face. She was a glimpse of light, disappearing. A fleeting glow at a shaft head. An aurora, half-imagined by men who spent their lives in the dark.

And so, Callum came not to believe. He passed a year in the

mine, then two. His soft hands became sore, then red, then leather, until his pick was part of his body and its motion the rhythm of his life. Two years became three, four. And then one day, as Callum put down the pick and listed along the drift, carrying the day's handful of ore dust to the surface, he saw the light ahead. It struck the rock rib in a buttery splash, suggesting a form that was gown and waist and tapering neck. Then, it was gone. Callum froze, belief flooding him with gooseflesh. He touched the rock to leave the story behind. She was real. He had seen the Lady with the Lantern.

Then the years became five, then eight and ten. Other boys were called and Callum became a man. His plot was three feet deep now, and he climbed its dark wall each day to dig the ore. When he was not in the mine, he barely thought of it. Life was comfortable. Soon, he had a wife, then a son. But when he entered the portal, he thought nothing of them. There was only the ore, and the rock-soaked stories of the Lady with the Lantern. Sometimes, a month would pass without a sighting; sometimes, it was three. Between times, rock would fall, men would be lost. And always, at day beginning and end, Callum rode the lift to the portal.

One day, after twelve years, the rocks took Callum's father when they fell. Callum was four feet down in his plot when he learnt through his fingertips. And then he was empty. For a week, he came and went at the portal, sold his ore, played with his son, every action echoing hollow around his chest. Until anger filled the void. The Lady with the Lantern could have saved him; should have. He wanted to know who she was, how she was. His fingers groped angrily at the plot walls, pulling out every story. And still, she was nothing but a light, and a flash of hair. Featureless, a blank face, always out of sight.

Eighteen years came and went, and one day, Callum found his son's steps behind him. He wanted to speak, but they were through the portal and words flowed only through the rock. He sensed the boy learning the thing he had learned, and was powerless to stop it.

Time seemed to gather pace, one day interred in another. Callum climbed the six feet into his plot each morning. He had long ago ceased to bring a head lamp; every dusty surface as familiar as skin. But when the day was nearly gone, he saw his arm, and then his pick, slowly gathering light between the dust. He straightened and tipped his head. And she was standing above him.

He saw the lantern first, its lead-light faces breaking the light into bars. Then, the edge of her skirt, dusty and worn. His heart thundered and he reached for the rock, ready to speak her face into the stories of the mine. Instead, she shifted the lantern, and he could speak no more. She had no nose, no mouth, and her eyes were pits, empty, pale and lashless. She pointed her finger at his chest, and he saw it was bones as white as her flesh.

She spoke through her nothing mouth. *The debt is paid.*

Callum let down his pick. His voice came from the rock, hollow and wrong within the narrow plot. *What debt?*

Your father's.

Callum thought a long time. About the ore he had mined, that his father had before. That his son did even now. All the men … the mine … and the darkness. Her light made his skin heavy; he was tired. His life only now made sense. *And mine?* he asked.

She swung the light forward. *That is for your son.*

And so, Callum laid down on the floor of his plot, as long as he was, and deep enough. He reached for the wall, but there was no time to tell of the Lady's face. The mine shuddered, the roof came down, and the lantern was lost behind the rock.

THE GHOST OF HEPHAESTUS

Shortlisted for the Aurealis Award for Best Fantasy Short Story
Shortlisted for the Ditmar Award for Best Novella or Novelette

The knock comes at midnight.

He draws himself from his crumbling books, his limbs coiled to run, his stockinged feet silent on the boards. The candles have burned to stubs, captive flames glittering within the hundred glass jars, trapped behind the pitch sheet in the window. He edges to the shop door, lace quivering at his wrist, his eyes falling on the false panel behind the apothecary's mortar. Will he have time to throw the latch if it is Kelvin's men?

But the gas-lit spy glass mirror reflects a cascade of golden hair upon the threshold.

No! It is *her*.

Heat from a phantom furnace flushes upon his face. He fumbles with the locks and throws the door into the frosty night. A moan catches in his chest. She slumps against the frame, her garment barely a night-slip, a soft linen cascade, ineffectual against the thick cold. She turns her eyes up, their orbits sunken, her lips blue and cracked.

Her voice is a ragged wisp of fog. "Physician. I am dying."

He knows not who she is. She has come to him before, but always in the daylight, her hair caught under a hat, her clothes and face both fine and foreign. She has asked of him strange things. Did he stock a rendered fat for greasing cogs? Her accent had whispered around his other customers, tendrils that had made a memory of her amongst dozens. He'd pointed her to the machinists, but she had told him their stock was unclean. Purity was what she craved; every time the same. He thought her vain at first, a high lady seeking to stall the turn of the clock with potions.

But he noted how she moved. In the bend of her arm and the tilt of her head, she was smooth as grace. More keenly he watched, each time she came to move amongst his shelves. Something inhuman. Something … beautiful.

So, while the sane part of him knew she must be nothing more than an exotic woman, unfamiliar, he imagined her the embodiment of the statements that had struck him from the Society, that had made him the target of Kelvin's men. And one day, after her gloved hand brushed his in the exchange of coins, he dreamed of her—her insides driven on gears and coils, stoked with blue fire, driven on closed circuit steam. He woke sweating, as if the steam were beside him in his bed.

As if his madness were real.

And now, she is here on his doorstep.

Trouble etches in his thoughts as he draws her inside, but he shoves the dream-maddened picture of her from his mind. He stokes the fire with her laid on the threadbare chaise. Her skin is chilled. He feels for her pulse and finds it curious: surging then shuddering with tiny thrills. Perhaps her heart? Then his eyes fall upon the yellowish bruise, a stain spreading from her gracious throat into the scooped neck of her garment. Lord, had she been struck? Is she bleeding inside?

"Lady," he prompts, his hands on her slender shoulders, his mind searching his stocks for curative powders. "Have you fallen?" No response. "Beaten?" Nothing. "What has done this to you?"

Her lips lift then, sad, a ghost of loss. Her hands move, fluid, one final act. He moves to stop her, thinking she means to uncover herself, but the reality is a greater shock. She taps atop her collarbone, and the panel of her chest unfolds.

He falls to the floor in shock, and sees his dream incarnate.

Inside, she is not a woman of bones and blood. Her chest is caged in the dull glint of forged silver. A pump turns beneath, feeding a tangle of pipes, finger-thick to hair fine, each peristalsing in the rhythm of her pulse. Where muscle should have lain are cables of telescoping steel. His hand creeps across his mouth, as if the sight of her has not already rendered him speechless. He rests there, in dull unmoving thought, reality absorbing as slowly as water into oiled cloth.

It takes him a long time to notice the imperfections, but then come many. That there is rust, that one of the telescopes contracted and seized. Another has been removed, its neat cable replaced with a cumbersome, worn sprocket and chain. And one of the pipes is split, weeping straw-colored fluid; a leak surges with each beat of the pump. His other senses return. He sniffs, recognizing the delicate oil he has sold her before. Oil in her steel veins. The *whirr* and *click* of the pump against its silver cage. A gurgle growing louder. The struggling sound of danger.

Physician, I am dying.

He no longer knows whether he is waking or sleeping. Perhaps his head has fallen on his work desk and soon he will stir. But until that moment, he rummages in his instruments and jars. He stems the leak with sticky gum of a plum tree, then binds the break with gauze soaked in paraffin. Then gently, in the terror of unchartered territory, he cleans the internals of the slippery fluid. When he is done, she has still not woken, so his eyes fall on the worn replacement sprocket. In a fit, he dashes the internals of his mantle clock and finds a cog to match. He cuts his finger in replacing it, red blood against gold and silver. Then finally, when her pulse has not improved, he digs in a dusty drawer for his transfusion kit. He hesitates. He knows that physicians have transfused before, but it is often death. And this is not blood.

He shakes himself and sinks his needle through the chain-mail of her pipework, finer links than what his eye can see, and hangs his last bottle of oil. And his own waking never comes, as if he is not dreaming after all.

He hears the pre-dawn birds before she wakes. She draws her

knees up, her chest panel closed now, the fading bruise the only sign of what has transpired. She is a woman again, but more beautiful to him now than before. A face a sculptor would render in stone, like the Elgin marbles he's stood before in the London museum. The delicate smell of the oil hangs in the air, like the discomfort between them now. He breathes as little as possible, hoping to prolong the dream.

"How do you feel?" he asks.

"As before," she says, her fingers opening and closing. "Tired. Stiff. Failing." The last is a whisper.

He closes his eyes, imagining it is the time to awake now, but the world persists. "I've dreamed of you," he says, stupidly, as if he is courting her. "Are you real?"

Alarm flies into her face. Her eyes dart to the blackened window, as if she hears boot steps. "What did you see?"

He shakes his head. "Just … what you are."

She swings her feet down. Her gaze falls fearfully on the door. "I must leave."

"My lady, did someone hurt you?" he asks, a protective fire lighting in his chest. He knows what it is like to have enemies.

She levels her stare on him. "I don't want to die."

"But, my lady, you are machine. How will you ever die?" The words echo in his skull. He has said words like them once, to the Royal Society. To Lord Kelvin. Of marriage of man and machines. They are the words that have made him an outcast, in fear of his life. And if they knew of her … he can only wonder what she faces.

He drops his voice. "Is it Kelvin's men after you, also?"

She springs towards the door. At the last moment, she stops. "I thank you, Physician."

And then she is gone. He turns to his shop, upended, jars open, the air thick with oil and spice. The cog he removed rests in a slick puddle. Ponderously, he cleans it, until the surface is bright. Until he sees the marks on the metal. He pulls the pitch sheet from the window and throws the disc into the sunlight. Letters. Frantic, as though they will fade, he rummages his desk for a lens. Astonishingly small, he scans them, his mouth moving over familiar script. Greek, he is sure of it. Alpha, omega, eta. But he cannot translate it.

He stares at the mess in his shop, marks the cleaning before he can open, aware how this everyday has paled against thoughts of what wonders are being done in Greece.

A week passes, full of customers, of tinctures, of remedies and advices sought. Twice, thick men in bowler hats take turns about the shop, inspecting the jars and buying nothing. He affects an air of aloofness, watches them while explaining the administration of cod liver oil to a lady's maid, or frowning into his mortar, but his thoughts stutter with his heart. These men smell of the docks, of dirty taverns and greasy money for intimidation. The second time such men thump their boots around his floor, a pressure reaches a limit within him. He is not a man of inaction. He throws the bolt to closed, collects his hat, and strikes out for London's heart. He can think of only one place to go, and it is a long time since he dared.

Around carriages, beneath gas lamps, over cobbles and tortuous lanes, he strides with the small package in his fist. Melting from the evening crowds, he enters the seminary's peace and seeks the chapel, avoiding the next door building with its hulking facade and unpleasant history. And there, in the chapel pew, as expected, he finds Terrance on his knees before God.

He waits in the back pew until Terrance rises and smiles, his hair already gray, his face soft with reverence and betraying no surprise. They fall into silent step towards the library.

"John, my friend," says Terrance, as if they have not had many years separated by their ideals and differing views. "What have you brought me?"

John fumbles in his pocket for the packet and lens, and a moment later, Terrance is regarding the script in a manuscript light.

"It's Greek, yes?" he asks Terrance. "Can you tell me what it says?"

Terrance frowns. "Greek, yes. I'll need to consult my notes. Where did you get this, from some scrap?"

John frowns and avoids the question, and makes his excuses. Terrance copies the text and John escapes into the London night, the cog safe in his fingers, the secret safe in his chest.

For three days, he expects Terrance to send word, and none comes. Each day, he opens and closes the apothecary, feeling his memories of her dusting over, like abandoned furniture in a stately house. But after the fourth day's sunset blush, when he has closed and retreated behind the pitch, a knock finally comes.

Terrance.

But, no.

He finds her on the doorstep again, dressed this time, her lip in her teeth. He holds the door open, his heart thudding in a lover's rhythm. She drifts to the chaise, then shies as if dodging its memory. Stretches her hands to the fire. Nervous.

He closes the door. "Are you followed?"

She shakes her head. "At least, I think not. Artemis's dogs are swift and silent."

He cocks his head. "Artemis's dogs—?"

"I am afraid, Physician."

"Of whom?"

"Of the others. Of the fire bird. Of the end times."

In his line of work, he has seen many with illnesses of the mind, and these words are like theirs. Words erupted above white stretched shirts, beneath brows greasy with imagined fears. Perhaps he has imagined the whole, crazed story, too. But she has not the cast of those types. His fingers settle on the cog, still in his pocket. He draws it out and shows her.

"I didn't imagine you, did I? You are real?"

Her nod is sharp. "And once flesh, like you."

"Then who did this to you?"

The question paints terror in her features. "I must go."

And she flies from the shop before he can stop her. His questions tumble over themselves. If she was once flesh, then someone has transformed her. Someone knows what he wants to know; the juncture of man and machine, the Darwinian cheat, the key of immortality.

So when another knock comes, he leaps up, hoping she has returned, only to find Terrance on the stoop.

"It's Greek," he confirms, shaking evening drizzle from his flat cap. "But not modern. Not even biblical. Ancient. Someone has played a joke on you, John. A student, perhaps. Unless you've been playing in the digs."

"What does it say?"

"It says, *Made by the hands of Hephaestus.*" Then Terrance glances around the shop with its jars of potions and powders. His face darkens, his thoughts as clear as if he had spoken: all this is a testament, man's attempt to thwart the will of God with medicine and science. To dismiss prayer and acceptance. Terrance is soon gone, the rekindled accord fizzling in his wake.

But John has what he wants. Hephaestus. He knows that name, learnt on the hard benches of his schooling. A god of the ancient pantheon. He pulls a dusty text from his shelf and sits heavily on the chaise. *Hephaestus, a smith god.* And now some great inventor has taken the name. John reads, his blood thundering. *God also of metal and fires and craftsmen. Created the weapons of the gods. Married to Aphrodite, later Aglaea.* He reads on, of automatons built to work the forges. Of the winged sandals of Hermes, of Achilles' armor.

This is mythology. Made-up gods and made-up faith, like the arguments that split he and Terrance apart. He slams the book with a shudder of dust, his thoughts balanced on a thin edge. Then he decides.

She is no myth. He has repaired her, heard her words. Smelled her skin. So this Hephaestus … he too must be real.

When she comes again, he knows it was not by choice. Her arm has seized, and it changes her fluid walk into a stare-drawing shuffle. She doesn't have to ask. He sits her on the chaise and gathers what tools he has. She stares at the high corner of the room, tears brimming.

"I am an apothecary," he says gently, before he begins. "I know not what I am doing. Should you not find someone who knows this work? Return to Greece, perhaps?"

"There is no one who knows this work, not anymore," she says.

"Hephaestus?" he tries. But even as the word leaves him, he

senses the tension tugging through her skin. This name has meant something awful to her.

"He is dead." Her voice is flat and final.

A pressure forms behind his breastbone. A master craftsman, gone. Someone with the name of a god, with god-like craft. "That's a shame," he says.

Her face hardens. "It is a *sign*. Gods do not *die*."

He tries to take a breath and finds himself paralyzed. It is as though he is speaking with Terrance again, things taken seriously that are not real.

"The firebird is building its bower," she goes on. "If I die, the Age will end."

Here are words again that speak to him of madness. And he would think her mad, if he didn't know she was a machine. If this situation were not mad enough already. If he had not decided to attach himself to her.

He tries escape through reason. "But how can you know this? Even if the world was to end—"

"The Age, not the world," she corrects him. She pauses, then, "When I was young, long ago, I saw things to come. I saw that I would die. Now the others want to force me to look again."

"The others?"

"Zeus, Artemis … and Aphrodite." She says the last name with poison of long regret. He feels the burrs of her emotion catch on him, draw chills along his skin and cut inside his stomach. He tries to tell himself she must be from a family beloved of old stories, whose children were named for imaginary beings long past. But some thin tendril of thought within him knows this is not truth. A dozen times he tries to retreat into the paradigm of the world before he knew her, and he finds he no longer fits through the door. He is in a bleak open plain of thought. A brisk wind pushes against his doubt and his reason.

"What is your name?" he asks, tremulous.

"I am Aglaea."

He reaches a hand towards her, to make her real, but she cowers back. "You should not touch my skin, or you may see the future, too."

The last shreds of disbelief tear away.

There is almost nothing written of her. He pours through his meager texts while she watches the flames crackling in the grate. The air is still scented with the delicate oil, the winter frost lurking in the room's distant edges.

"You are one of the Graces," he says, lowering the last volume. "Your name means 'splendor'."

The air shifts as she settles behind his shoulder. A curious thrill steals across his skin.

"What else does it say?"

"Not much. You were married to Hephaestus—"

"Never." Her voice is a knife through the very idea.

He clears his throat. "I am sorry, the sources conflict. Others say Aphrodite, though it was not a good match … she teased his deformities." Aglaea sighs. He goes on, "And you were her attendant?"

A bitter laugh. "Your books are so simple, Physician. This was not how it was."

He twists from his seat on the floor, looks up into her face. She is splendor to him, both the lilt of her voice, the cast of her features, and the machine within. If this book is not truth, then he wants it from her. Wants to understand how to help her. "Then how was it?"

She hesitates, her gaze falling on her hands. "I can show you, Physician. But what you see will be long past. You risk your mind remaining in the ether."

The term settles within him like a swallowed stone. "Lord Kelvin believes in the ether. It has led to quintessence, on which the ill-studied physician relies. It is not real."

She raises her hands. "It is the river from the past to the future, the place of all memory. It is real enough."

Her hands fall on his shoulders.

His ears pop; he is falling. The ground rushes to meet him, expanding as a great white hall lined with fire pits and benches. He slaps his hands over his ears: hammers pound, hot metal hisses in buckets, furnaces roar, and all echoes amongst the marble.

Then, he hears her voice in his ear. "This is the work hall." The noise dims.

He stumbles amongst the benches. On some are swords of fine construction. On others, shields, javelins, breastplates and greaves. Behind each bench and forge toils an automaton, dull with soot but tireless, performing the same moves again and again. He reels on, afraid of something ahead without knowing why. He reaches the end where three forges stand apart. Here are parts he recognizes. Silver ribcages, in different stages of design. Fine braided tube. Pumps, such as he has seen in Aglaea's chest. He stops.

"Keep moving," she hisses.

Then he sees ahead. Two figures stand by a screen in the hall's side, far from the noise of the forges. A lady, and a man. *No, not a man.*

John absorbs the detail. The twist of this figure's leg, the power in his hands and shoulders. He hears a voice in his head, as if the ether has spoken: *Hephaestus. A god.* Beside this god, he recognizes Aglaea, in a floating robe, melancholy drooping her shoulders like a shawl. Hephaestus grips her arm and draws her towards the screen. Anger surges within John, but the hands on his shoulders keep him still. "It is a memory, only," she says, though her voice is choked.

John drifts around, to where he can see their faces. Hephaestus' smile is a slash across his face, grim and satisfied. Aglaea is the mask of misery. They stare through a screen as fine as muslin, but as rigid as glass. With shock John registers the scene. Another man. *No, a god.* Full-armored, ravishing a woman in a twist of scarlet sheets. *Aphrodite.*

Hephaestus forces Aglaea forward. "Look," he murmurs. "Magnificence."

Aglaea averts her eyes, but Hephaestus is locked. "Beauty like that, I can give you," he says, running a finger down Aglaea's cheek as the debauchery plays out. "Tonight. Forever. It will work this time. And you will be mine, then. And you will tell me what you have seen."

And despite the obscenity, despite the shame of this, he sees the lift at the corners of her eyes. *Hope.* Just before she glances to the hall's end, where two memorials lie side by side. *Fear.*

As if the ether has catalyzed thought, John understands: Aglaea loved Hephaestus, enough to allow him to transform her body. Even when he had killed her sisters perfecting his technique. Even when he taunts her with hope.

John's hands curl and compress, emotion feeding a furnace inside his head. Then he is stumbling, the hall turning over. A rush of cold and darkness. Pressure on his cheeks, then on his legs, the crackling heat of the fire on his face. His world returns.

"Physician?" Aglaea's voice, ribboned with concern.

He holds himself still as the nausea rolls through his guts and thoughts, as if an invisible hand is hauling both into his mouth. He thinks of curative ginger and peppermint, but this is more than sickness. The link between his mind and body feels tight and frayed, ready to snap. Her hands brush his coatsleeves, soothing. *It is the ether, let it go.* He is not sure whether she is speaking, or if the voice is still in his head. He fights against the phantom organ thief, feeling his mind towed towards insubstance. *Let it go!*

He gives in, prepares himself to empty his stomach, but instead the sensation slips away. His body is real again. Stiff and bruised, he turns to her worried gaze.

"You mustn't hold onto the ether," she warns him.

But he is remembering what he has seen in those brief minutes of memory, glimpsing the depths of her torment. His own self diminishes. He doesn't need to ask why she allowed Hephaestus to change her. But he wants to know what happens now; his part in it. How he protects her. "What did he want you to show him?"

She retracts, but not as far as before, long fingers unfolding, mechanically smooth, against her chin. "What will come to pass."

He scrambles to his knees, and takes her hands in his. "And what is that?"

She bites her lip, tiny white teeth.

He implores her, even as he feels the ether pull at him again through her skin. "Please?"

It comes in a rush. "His death. And mine—"

From outside comes the splash of a cartwheel sunk in a puddle. Her eyes snap to the window, widening like a doe caught in the open. Crawling dread claws his skin as he follows her gaze. In his silent stockings, he creeps away from the fire, towards the pitch-black window. Nothing seems amiss; all the smells are familiar, the sounds of a usual night. But something, *something*…

With trembling fingers, he tears the black sheet from the

window. He catches twin lights of slit-centered eyes, the twin bloom of hot breath against the glass, the white flash of a fang. Then, nothing. He stands, stilling his thundering heart, knowing in his ancient brain, the parts Darwin's processes have never touched, that she has been hunted and tracked here.

Artemis's dogs are swift and silent.

Eventually, he replaces the pitch and returns to the chaise. He looks on her, in her flowing robes, every inch a woman. Every part a machine. Every inch within his heart.

"You should stay here," he says.

He cannot avoid his duties. While Aglaea remains in his loft room, he runs the shop in a haze of diminished importance. A week passes this way, and never again does he see the phantom hunting beast, nor sense its presence. Yet every day when he closes, he takes his ancient hunting stick and sweeps around the cobbled streets, returning only when chilled in breath and skin, and he can watch over Aglaea sleeping on his chaise.

Then, there are the repairs. Every day, something in her workings breaks or seizes, and he fixes her as best he can. He asks her why the parts are failing, so obviously well made. A bloom has crept across all the metal within her now. Why is that? She will not speak of it. And so, as each time seems to risk her very existence, a disquiet grows within that he must remedy before he can sleep.

His circles grow wider. Once, he imagines he sees a woman in robes at the mouth of a lane, her hair caught like a marbled statue, a quiver over her shoulder, a stag by her feet. When he blinks, she is nothing but a crone with an overladen basket, a scowl on her face for his stare and her lamp-lit shadow suggesting a deer. He curses himself, but he can't help it. He mis-sees the robed woman again, and again. Sometimes alone, and sometimes with another: a woman tangled with roses who disappears into sparrows or swans.

He does not tell Aglaea. Finally, after ten days, his widening circle reaches a certain street and he stops. The church spires rise into the darkening night, set afore the full moon. He creeps to the gate and sets his hands about the bars. Buttery light leaks from the chapel windows, a dozen helpful candles. He catches movement to his side. A glance shows him another robe-clad woman, a snake twisted on her arm this time, an owl with glowing eyes atop her head. The clean scent of lemons fills his nose. He shakes himself, looks again. A gaslight post draped with an abandoned harness piece is all he sees.

Is he losing his sanity?

He finds himself back at the Society's gates, looking for the logic he remembers in the yellow window squares. Instead, he rushes the gate to the adjoining churchyard and crawls into a back-row pew. He is a stranger amongst the faithful, but his real world is stranger still. He drops his head on his hands, in what must look like prayer.

Hours later, a hand touches his shoulder, and Terrance sinks alongside. His robes color the air with incense, drawing John's memory of Aglaea's scented oil.

"My friend," begins Terrance, as if their paths have gently re-met.

"I cast myself upon you," begins John, holding back the tide of words that want to rush off his tongue. "Will you hear the ravings of a mad man?"

Terrance takes his elbow. A glow of confidence settles within John. He glances to the alcoves, where the mysterious robed women wait in his peripheral vision, statues and flowers when he examines them directly. He sighs. And he tells Terrance everything, from the beginning of Aglaea to the end of these visions. Terrance listens patiently, perhaps the only man in the world who could hear this talk of gods and machines without assuming madness. Such delusions are his usual staple.

When John leaves later, it is with absolution. But as he treks towards the store, that lingering lemon scent burrows into his mind. He looks on Aglaea, uneasily slumbering on the chaise, he knows she is in pain constantly, now, as if all the things of which she will not speak are breaking her down. Vulnerable to what lives in her memories, in the future, in the night. And he can't help feel he has betrayed her confidence.

That he has been the one to truly place her in danger.

Three days later, something serious breaks within her. He hears the gasp from above floors, the thud as she impacts the floor. It is just before he closes for lunch, and the shop is silent, but for a delivery man who is complaining of thefts as he waits for his coins. He pays the man and rushes upstairs in a sweat of fear. He is quite unprepared. Not for the fact she is sprawled on the threadbare floor rug, her skin losing its rose like an autumn petal … no. It is the sickness in his breast that tells him how she has crept upon him, night by night as he has tended her. How her words and her suffering have bent his affection, until she means more to him than any object or patient he could see. Whether she is flesh or machine, it makes no difference. He loves her, now.

But he is losing her.

This time, she cannot tell him what has failed. He knows her mind is still flesh, and it has sunk under unconscious fog. He lifts the panel of her chest. All within is smirched in gray patina. He searches for leaking oil, for breakage in this anatomy of silent steel. Silent.

Her pump heart.

A chilly hand strokes his throat. The pump is not moving. Frantic, he puts his ear close, trying to hear around his own thundering pulse. Has something inside it caught and jammed?

He hears no clicks. And something else is wrong. The soft scented oil is too faint, her workings cool. The ribs tick and sigh, like a kettle retreating from boil.

He curses, and pushes back the lower panel, where the blue-fire boiler stares back, its pilot spot empty and cold.

The fire has gone out.

By now, he knows enough of her workings to understand this is not a fuel problem. Deep in her pelvis is a complex system of wonder that makes the blue fire from the things she eats. If he can relight the pilot, perhaps…

He strikes a match, but the old wick crumbles at the fire's touch. He throws the still-lit shaft aside, searching the room. An old sooted lamp rests atop the mantle. He splits his nails tearing the wick from its belly with his bare hands. The process seems to take an age: a knife to cut the length, threading the wick into her gold-hammered case, and touching the flame. And even when the light takes, he stands over her, his fist in his mouth, his heart hammering his senses. The boiler is hissing back to pressure, now, the pump in her chest turning again…but surely it has been too long? That cold stroking hand turns savage, twisting his own fleshy heart. What if she never wakes?

He has to watch for the whole afternoon, and the evening, and into the long blue hours of the night. Her color returns, but she does not stir until the witching hour, when he is wretched with inevitable grief. So when her hand drifts up to touch her face, the relief knocks him sideways. He grasps the hand.

"Thank God," he says, without thinking, and gathers her against him, fragrant again and whole. But worry has made up his mind. He looks into her half-open eyes. "You must tell me why this is happening. You must."

There is a long moment, where he feels the weight of all she is, all the time she has lived. Then she sighs. "The Age is ending, Physician."

"I don't understand."

She pushes herself up. "The world has Ages that renew after many, many years. The Olympians fear it."

"What will happen?" he whispers.

"The Titans will come. Everything changes."

"How do—"

"Because I saw it. Once. Long ago." Her eyes flicker over him, then soften. "My talent was not beauty, Physician. It was sight. What I allowed Hephaestus to do disguised me. I knew when the Age changed, I would die. A god always dies."

John hears her past words come back to him. "But Hephaestus died."

"Yes." The sound is like a door closing. "And when he died, his work began fading. So, the body he made is failing…" Her eyes fix on him, those lovely eyes that are still flesh. "Physician, please, you must keep me in repair. Stall the Age."

The chilly hand within John has a name now: helplessness. He shakes his head, slowly. He can hear how her breath catches. How she is steadily eroding within. Is it even right he should do what she asks? If he wasn't in love with her, if he wasn't in awe of what she was, would he want to?

"I don't know if I can," he says truthfully.

Her gaze widens. "You have never seen a Titan, Physician. You don't know what they will do to the world." Her voice softens, like the spent embers from a once-hot fire. "War and suffering … and I do not want to die."

His head is in his hands, now, his thoughts a tumble. "A few weeks ago, all this was fantasy," he says. "I did not believe in gods or Ages. I imagined men as machines … but not such as you are."

When he looks up again, her face has composed, and he senses the ether coursing through her skin. Where her hands rest on him, he feels its tug. "You do not believe it," she says. "Then I will show you."

She drags him from the shop, barely able to collect his coat against the heavy chill which stalks the city like a beast waiting to swallow the sunrise. And suddenly, he knows she is taking him towards Terrance's churchyard. They stop atop a broken cobble in a gas lamp's shroud.

"There," she says.

He looks and sees nothing different. The church, sleeping, its shingled roof and thrusting spire. The seminary slumped alongside. Somewhere in there dwells Terrance, but he knows not what she means. "I see nothing."

"*There.*" She grips his hand and his gaze drags upwards.

"I still—" But he does. In the ether's lens, he sees it. A tangle ringing the steeple top, coils and twists of thick sticks … no, not sticks. Wires. Metal shards. Coach suspension straps. And amongst it, he spies a beaked head, weaving. As they watch, the bird perches on the side of its savage nest, a tumbling vision of shimmering feathers, catching the first rays of dawn.

"Firebird," hissed Aglaea. "When the Age ends, she will burn to ashes and rise again."

He stares in wonder, the threads of these fantasies twisting into a knot he cannot unpick, not with his helpless hands. "Then what can you do?" he asks.

She glances around, and he has the sense he has felt many times before on his walks, of women in robes in the edges of shadows.

Her face hardens, and in the hiss of her breath he hears *Aphrodite*, and from the beat of the ether in his skin, he knows she is speaking to someone else in ways he cannot hear.

The sunrise is complete before she answers his question. She does it with her hands on the sides of his face, her gaze imploring, pulling every string of his marionette heart. "You must repair me, Physician. And keep me hidden. The firebird has only a day to wait for the fire after it finishes its nest, or it will die and not rise again. Keep me safe until then."

But an unease has planted itself in his senses, and nothing will shift it. His walks take him back to the church, not to Terrance, now, but to see the growing bower of the firebird, near complete. The robed figures are in his dreams now. They circle the store at night, and hot breath blows on the window panes. And the unrest seems to extend to everything else. Clouds rush across the sky, and the weather turns warm. People visiting his shop creep in, their voices soft. Word comes of fights in the streets, not just at the docks, but in Mayfair. For the first time, he takes down his hunting rifle and leans it by the door. And when a knock comes one evening, when Aglaea is in the grip of slumber after another repair, his eyes stroke that long, greased barrel and he wonders if a man with a bowler hat is on his step … or a beast with steaming breath.

It is neither.

A woman blocks the fading light, her coat golden, its hood drawn about her face. She is taller than he is, commanding. He feels a shudder, made of robed phantoms that stalk his moves.

"Who are you?" he demands, his eyes raking the dark for glowing eyes or bared teeth. The ether whispers a name to him, but he does not catch it.

"Admit me, Physician. I am not here to harm you. Or the Grace."

His eyes settle on the golden snake circling her throat, and his limbs move against his will. He holds the door for her, then closes out the night. He follows her as she moves to the center of his floor, ringed with shelves and jars and powders. He feels her gaze as a measuring weight, assessing what he is worth.

"Why are you here?" he croaks.

"You must not protect her," says the figure.

Rage sparkles within him, fanned by the helpless hand. "Do not tell me what to do."

She sighs. "Your heart has been touched. It will not be easy. But you must let her go."

"What do you know of it?" he demands.

She raises her hands, as if she is a merchant's scale. "Only certainty. The Age will change, but not without the firebird. She must have the courage to face her fate."

"Why does she have to die?"

The figure shakes her head. "Only she knows that, if she has looked. She should never have submitted to Hephaestus. He was nothing compared to her. Even the Olympians cannot see the future. It is a gift she has run from too long. And if I knew, I could not speak of it. Such is forbidden, for it changes the path."

"Let them come for her, then," he says, the bravado of his firearm infecting his words.

"She knows how to disguise herself, Physician. We can do nothing to intervene, and you should not either. Let this take its course."

These words are like darts, with the same sharp tips Terrance's arguments used to dig in his breast. His tongue moves to ask her again who she is, how she dares to come here, and how does she know this at all? But the ether whispers her name again, and this time he hears it. *Athena. Justice.* No doubt can be a cloak enough for her.

Athena nods, sadly. "Civilization is teetering, Physician. No one sees it coming. The firebird has nearly finished. If it dies without the fire, the world cannot be reborn and the Titans will crack it open." She looks him up and down, and he feels as transparent as his powder jars. "You are not a man of faith, Physician, but you do not have to be. You have seen for yourself. Think on it, and swiftly."

When she is gone, he climbs the stair to look on Aglaea. Whether the world is ending or not, his life will end when hers does. He rakes over these feelings like coals, again and again, feeling the bright hurts of possibilities lost.

He needs time to cure himself, before he can decide what to do.

Perhaps, in a day, he can do it.

He stalls through the next turn of the sun, planning to lay this all before Aglaea when he closes. They will make a plan.

It all falls when the bowler-hat men break down his door. He has an instant to curse himself, for he has forgotten Kelvin amongst everything else.

"John Hector Battersby," says one thug, with an even grin. "Lord Kelvin wants to speak with you. And your *lady friend.*"

John is too far from the rifle. "You have no authority," he says, his knuckles white on his mortar's edges.

"We don't need any."

Then John sees the figure trailing the men on the street. Terrance. His cowl pulled up, his countenance serene. And he sees how all this has played out. The things he has told Terrance, about Aglaea, about his own disgrace with Kelvin and the Society.

As they drag him outside, he hears their footsteps on his stairs, knows they will soon have Aglaea, too. He clutches at Terrance's robes. "Why?" he hisses.

Terrance shakes him off, looks down his long nose with eyes of the wounded that say, *Never ask a man to choose between another man and his God.*

They take them to the Society, to a long thin room with a single window and a heavy door. Through the pane, he can see the church spire and the firebird, its work now complete under a slate-gray sky. A drum of thunder plays out across the heavens. He has the sense of events unraveling, now, and distant shouts of unsettled crowds. The room's sputtering candle reveals Aglaea slumped beside him, both of them tied in their chairs.

For several hours, they are abandoned. He works fruitlessly at the knots as night descends, as Aglaea sinks towards mechanical death. She mutters about forges, about sleeping and waking transformed, of Aphrodite and of Artemis's dogs. His senses scream to touch her, to find the fault that is turning her skin pale and blue. The ether brushes over him, turning his existence into a focused spot within a foggy dream. He realizes she isn't speaking out loud. He can hear her in his head.

Lord Kelvin comes to inspect them, cheerful in his great coat, and opens Aglaea's panels in a manner that drives John to dreams of his own, where he tears the man's eyes out with his fingernails. And then worse. Kelvin notices her poor condition, and he brings two men in overalls, who haul her away.

He screams himself voiceless, but Kelvin, unmoved, takes the vacated chair and sits opposite, his steely eyes and commanding mouth both working. "Battersby," he begins. "How did you do it?"

He refuses to answer.

Kelvin dabs his brow. "No matter. We will discover the secrets in time. You, on the other hand … the church will take care of you."

The storm's thunder rolls over them again. John tips his head to see the firebird outlined on the steeple. Ether crackles inside his skull. He can sense Aglaea, nearby. And others. The candle flickers and for a brief second, its flame splits in two.

"I care not for the church," he says.

Kelvin snorts. "But many do. And they will see your name smeared in improperness. Your shop will be cast down. Unless …" He raises a gray brow.

Unless you give me your secrets. John hears the unspoken question in ether-speak. He knows he has none to give. He has been nothing in these events but a leaf caught in Aglaea's eddy. A sadness settles inside him. No one will know what he has felt. Is it still noble? Does it still matter, even so?

But Kelvin doesn't know this. With his last discipline, John affects a ponderous face. "Perhaps I can show you. Take me to her."

They have her on a long surgeon's table, machinists prodding about in her insides. This room's windows are larger, and open onto the church. The storm grumbles. John's feet seem slow to him, each step a minute's passing. Ether sneaks about him, and his corner vision fills. They are all here, now. Robed figures, waiting for the end of the Age. He hears Kelvin's boots behind him, but all he sees is Aglaea.

The machinists have run tubes, turning hand pumps to prolong her life. Her eyes are closed, her head tipped, but he feels her pain in the tug of her mouth, in the twist of his own heart.

This is not a way to live.

Kelvin is asking him questions, and he sees his chance. He steps close. His mouth is working, spilling lies about metalworking techniques, about things he saw in Hephaestus's forge. But all he needs is to reach …

He gestures towards her pump, her silver ribcage, his heart breaking across the scale of rust and decay. His gaze fixes on the small tap below the blue-fire boiler. A collective breath draws, the ether pulls taut, the stormy sky roils. *Forgive me*, he thinks.

His fingers slip, then turn, and her blue-fire fuel slicks away. The boiler shudders, the wick blows out.

It seems to take forever as she holds on, but then the pump slows and ceases. Yelling. Kelvin's men realize the demise. He feels a fist connect his jaw, driving his consciousness into momentary retreat. The floor is rushing up to meet him, but he never feels the impact.

Instead, he feels the *pull*. It's the sensation of a rope within his hands, dragging him into the sea. *Let it go.* He hears Aglaea's words again, but in Athena's voice. And then he knows: it's Aglaea who is streaming away, part of the ether herself. He feels himself rising, then looks down on his own body far below. Kelvin and the men are working, but Aglaea is gone; what remains only a machine.

And through the window, the sky looses a bolt, shattering the church spire. The lightning sets the firebird's nest aflame.

Pandemonium.

He hears the monks erupt from their worship, the shouts from Kelvin and his men. And his own grip on the skyward pull slowly slips. Panicked, he feels Aglaea's gentle touch on his shoulders, as it was in Hephaestus's forge.

I am not dying, Physician.

But I am, he thinks. He can feel the tie to his body stretching tight, soon to fray and snap.

The Age is turning, she says. *War is coming. And a time when the ether will drive the world. Let go, Physician. Live to see it.*

He grasps for her hand. Feels the last touch of her skin, the last scent of the delicate oil. Then his mind loses grip.

When he comes to, he is in the churchyard, the spire ablaze on the last of twilight. Someone thrusts a pail into his fist and he ferries water like a machine himself. But the blaze is ferocious, and all through the night it consumes the church, pushing back any who come near. He watches, stunned, from the gas lamp post, the fire pushing away the cold blanket night. Until dawn when all that remains is lingering coals, and ash paler than snow.

He slumps before it in a daze, a thick tear unshed in his eye. A shadow falls, and he stares up at a tall, hooded woman, the snake necklace glowing in the pale light.

Physician.

He cannot assemble his thoughts. His voice is a croak, battered with night and loss. "She is gone."

Not gone. Transformed. As she should have been.

He wipes his nose on his sleeve like a child. Transformed or lost, both the same and neither a comfort. Athena serves him the neutral smile, of justice, of things made right.

Remember you have touched the ether, Physician. You will see her again.

The air shifts, and he knows the goddess is gone. He hauls himself up on the lamp post. The sun is sneaking above the buildings, now. And against its bloom is a bird, rising, its feathers streaming fire.

JACK

West End, London, 1924

James Kelly's boots had scarce touched English soil again before he found himself drenched in the gorrawful wailing Jazz that had so infected New York. The West End rain was doing its fair best to compete; yet the Jazz was winning, and spawning all manner of vain, painted, sleeveless forms dribbling about the pavement.

"Well, hey cutie, don't you look the big cheese?"

James started with the horror of being snuck upon, and by one of the dribbles, a blue-eye painted harlot dripping pearls onto a filmy shift barely passing for an undergarment. Her scarlet red mouth gave him a sassy, tight-slipped smile. James shrugged his shoulders inside his suit-jacket, shifted his necktie as if he might just be taking directions. But he put his hand in his pocket, covering his valuables lest this whore try to lift them. He was a man given to judgments, which his own mother had not enjoyed and his late wife even less, but he remained self-assured in his disposition despite the places it had led. A man of sixty-four was quite entitled to whatever vice he wanted.

"I'm fine, thank you," he said brusquely, and almost moved away but for the fact he had presently nowhere fixed to go. The harlot lifted her chin to the Jazz-infested club growing up from the foundations behind her. James supposed she was an employee, walking the curb to bring in the business.

"You in for some hooch, baby? Play a little snuggle pot?" she suggested, winking, and undeterred. She had an American accent. She lit a cigarette, and had eyes like a cat in the match-strike.

James certainly could use a drink, the chief reason for his return from the States where prohibition was tiresome for a man partial to both scotch and High Morals. He'd avoided the East End, because he'd known and hated it before going across the Atlantic. He was not policeman or priest, but his mind walked a narrow road. He did not frequent the houses of whores, he made his opinion known on the subject. But he was somehow drawn to moral corruption, as if to see how close he could dance to the fire before it caught him alight. He was a man with a powder keg core, but his fuse length was different every time. And that was part of the allure.

He wavered, and looked towards the club, at the slip-clad bodies hanging out of windows and dancing masses in splattered half-light. The place was cast in the New York speakeasy mold, but legal in prohibition-spared London. Again, he scrutinized the harlot from her dark bob and no-teeth smile, all the way down her slender bangle-ringed arms that finished in deep red nails.

"Hooch?" she whispered coyly, knowing him more plainly than he would admit. That got his fuse started.

"Alright," he said stiffly.

"Follow me," she said, leading him into the fray.

She told him her name was Mae, installed him at the bar and pressed into his hand a scotch glass tinkling with fresh ice. James found once one was in the middle of it all, the Jazz became a background he could ignore.

He perched on a high stool and looked about. The downstairs was overly dark, dotted here and there with gas lamps, one above each patron cluster. There were men about who looked, at least superficially, like himself. Business suits cut tight in the old style, neckties still done up, and being entertained by at least two flappers, each done up in slicker things than Mae and laughing uproariously between drags on dangling cigarettes.

James averted his eyes and took a bolt of Scotch and water. His fuse was burning, fanned by the whores' puffing cheeks, by their spines under their slip dresses. He didn't want to be excited by them, and was in danger of becoming so. He must muster his disapproval, so he tried to think of the inevitably awful whore's teeth behind Mae's tight-lipped smiles. He didn't think to notice a lack of young men; he was far too focused on censure and himself. But he did notice the drink on his second gulp.

"Hey, listen!" he bellowed indignantly at the bar. "This scotch is fair cut with water—!"

A girl behind the bar was over him in an instant, all copper hair pinned down with a feather band and big pale blue eyes.

"Shhhhh," she hissed, exuding menace that shut James's jaw with a hollow clank. He stared at her, trying to fix the problem he had with her features. At first, her nose was too long, then it was her lips, a shade too black to be pleasant. Then he took exception to her hairline, which was low on her brow and extended too far down her neck. Then, it was that she didn't blink. And yet, none of that was quite it.

"Is there a problem?" she asked, too aloof and loudly, as if knowing any problem was certainly trivial. James felt a brush against his suit sleeve and found all-lips-smiling Mae attached to his wrist. A few men looked up from their slapper hi-jinx, faces dazed and vaguely unhappy at interruption, until one of the girls recaptured their attention and they slammed home another hi-ball.

Mae squeezed his wrist, her nails digging in tight crescents of pain that only fanned his fuse. He put his hand in his pocket again, finding his valuables still in place, lowered his voice. "I can pay for the proper stuff," he said. He just wanted a damn drink. A stiff one. So the night wouldn't need to end as so many in the East End had.

Mae remained parasitically in place. "Our apologies," she soothed. "Lilian?"

Lilian reached for an under-bar bottle and filled his glass. James picked it up and threw back the shot while they watched him with their big, still eyes. The scotch was even weaker than the first, but James placed the glass back on the bar. Mae's nails were still at his wrist, pressed into the pulse.

He had a dark, involuntary thought in that moment, of a sharp blade and blood. He arrested it promptly with a more troubling notion: was this a Clip Joint? Like he'd heard tales of in New York?

Where they'd sell him watered whiskey and roll him later if he couldn't pay?

The ceiling bounced with dancers above, disrupting the thought. He looked again. This club wasn't busy enough, and these whores looked two potatoes from starving. They were milking profit, like all whores. Just the way it was. He pushed his glass forward.

"There you are, honey," said Mae approvingly. "Another?"

James nodded, but he started to look about. He wasn't afraid of this place, but he wanted to leave and without a scene. He was therefore startled, when he next looked up, to find the clock had moved itself three hours forward, the bar ringed with sweat from his mostly-ice glasses and laughter in his throat at something Mae had said. Even Lilian had lost sullenness in all the drink, though not the odd features. And still, she hadn't blinked.

Mae laughed again. "Well, Mr. Kelly, that's a riot! And you must have missed London handsomely, and it you!"

James's mouth smiled, but it was like someone else's face. He couldn't remember what the hell he'd told her—obviously something about his time in the States. "I suppose," he found himself saying. "But I didn't overly enjoy the East End. I won't go back there."

"Lilian's from the East End," said Mae. Then, "Were you in business there, Mr. Kelly?"

"Furniture and upholstery," said James. This was getting thoroughly out of hand. He had no desire to speak of anything about his life in London, the States, or anywhere between. Especially with whores. They should have been afraid of him, not enjoying extracting information.

He tipped himself off the stool. "I must be getting along," he declared.

The two girls exchanged a glance. "I'll get you the bill," said Lilian, diving off into a dark hole at the end of the bar.

James fished for his wallet. Distractedly as he dug, he looked around the room and found all the other men had vanished. He cursed himself even as he found his valuables. *This* was how depravity began. Getting cockeyed in a bar, too brave for sense, and who knew what would come after? Would he succumb and pay for their services? He was shaking, his fuse burning bright.

"Will we see you again, Mr. Kelly?" asked Mae, lips pressed and lifted in enquiry, handing back the jacket he couldn't recollect taking off.

Not on your life. But he smiled vaguely, wanting to be gone.

"There you are," said Lilian, pushing the hand-totted bill paper across the bar. James had to sit back on the stool, fuse momentarily forgotten. He squinted and added, and squinted again. But however he summed it, the bill was extraordinary, more than three weeks' wages. It *was* a Clip Joint. His resolve hardened faster than his sense.

"I'm not paying that!" he exclaimed. "That's extortion!"

"But Mr. Kelly, our rates are printed here quite clearly," said Mae, gesturing towards a creamy faced menu on the bar that James hadn't touched all night. "Private entertainments, drinks … all had by you."

"I'm not paying. I can't," said James finally, getting up from the stool.

"Well … that's just fine," said Mae slowly.

What happened next, James broadly felt, was a matter of drink telling him lies. For what he thought happened was that Lilian streaked across the bar and seized him by the collar. Then, these two slips of women dragged him out the back, down stairs into a dark room and sat him on a hard chair. A door closed and a lock turned, then he was alone with them and a single gas lamp.

"Who goes first?" It was Lilian, James knew that much.

"You, sister, of course," said Mae. "You have waited longer than me. I don't need it."

James's head cleared and he looked up. Neither woman was taking pains with their lips anymore, and both had brilliant white teeth. James therefore wondered why the no-teeth smiles, until Mae caught him looking and grinned.

"God damn!" cursed James. Mae had a pair of fangs, huge things nestled in her upper jaw. A quick look at Lilian and James decided she had 'em too. He went to bolt, and found himself tightly strapped. His illusion of whores and Clip Joints collapsed; the fuse went out. For comfort, he patted his pockets as far as the bindings would allow, and found that his valuables were, at least, still in place.

"I don't like him," Lilian was saying. "I've seen him before. Somewhere."

"Who cares?" demanded Mae. "Feed is feed. Do him and let him go. The drug'll wear off in an hour and then he won't remember at all."

Lilian folded her arms and pouted. "I don't trust him. Something ain't right."

"So watch his mind through the blood-sight! It lasts about as long as the drug and you can see where he goes and thinks. You'll make sure he doesn't tell anyone. You can't wait another day, sister."

"True enough," said Lilian. She leaned in to James's eye level, her pale blue irises tied to her eyeballs by a fine web of spidery blood vessels.

James wanted desperately to get his hands free. This close, creature or no, he still smelt a whore, a moral corruption poisoning the air. His fuse relit. "I can pay," he said, waggling his bound hands. "I'll pay. Let me pay."

"Sorry, honey, once you're back here, you can't pay with green, only red. Only an option to pay in the bar," said Mae.

"Definitely seen him before," said Lilian again.

James looked into her queerly conformed face. Yes, perhaps. He thought he might have seen her too, near forty years ago when he'd been a young man in the East End. Was she the one who'd come upon him that morning, in Whitechapel? Who'd startled him so that he'd run before finishing the work he'd been doing? He narrowed his eyes, remembering.

"Where did you live in the East End?" asked Lilian.

James kept his mouth shut. Fingered his pocket.

"Hurry up," demanded Mae. "Sun up's not far off and there's all the windows to board." When Lilian didn't move, Mae came around James and slipped a sharp finger inside his collar. His button and necktie fell open.

"Do it, or I'll kill him and neither of us gets any."

James swallowed, but didn't scream. This was all too surreal. A blunted reality he was sure couldn't exist. He told himself that right up until Lilian bit his neck. Then he could smell her skin, a rusty scent he'd had on his own fingers after handling old upholstery tacks.

It didn't last long and sounded like a cat drinking milk. There wasn't really any pain. James only became angry at the stuttered glimpses of consciousness. Whatever they'd put in the watery scotch was messing up his head. Mae was laughing at something, her pearls dancing, patting his cheek. Next thing, James found himself stumbling on the cobbles outside with a blur of early light touching the fog. His High Morals chose that moment to reassert themselves. Those women! He'd been used, taken in and done over, his own body imbibed and corrupted. They'd dragged him into their own immorality, and that made them worse than whores: they were monsters. And he knew how to deal with such things, as he had in the East End. His fuse burned through; the powder keg caught. They were monsters he knew from fiction: night creatures, day-sleepers, but it made no difference. His insides were on fire, and only blood could cool him.

So James reached into his pocket, past his wallet to the most valuable thing of all. He drew the scalpel into his hand and turned the handle over. The hard leather cover came away easily, revealing the sharp edge, nicked from heavy use and bright from polish.

Yes.

This was what London was to him, even more than New York. Cleaning house while his powder burned. Thirty years away had been too long.

Mae closed the last shutter and kicked her way happily through the off-cast wares of the night's dancers. Gloves, headbands, broken pearl strings. It was mess that spoke of money parted; besides, someone else would clean it while she slept. It had been a good night.

That was until she found Lilian, white and shaking, sitting on the bed in their windowless day-room.

"What?" she demanded.

"I told you I'd seen him before," said Lilian, in whispers. "In Whitechapel, forty years ago, you remember the killer? The Ripper?"

"Oh, you mean the thoughtful gentleman that made our activities so much easier?" said Mae, taking up a brush and starting on Lilian's hair. "Nothing like being able to actually drain them and blame someone else. Pull it together, Lil, you're boring me."

"I *saw* him doing it, Mae. Early before dawn one morning in Dutfield's yard. He killed a girl there with a scalpel, right through her throat. Then he saw me and ran."

"Fabulous convenience, I hope you drained her after he ran off." Mae brushed harder.

Lilian gave a small smile. There, that was more like it. She had. Mae was relieved her sister demonstrated such instinct.

Mae pressed on. "And yet you think it's the same man? After forty years, and he's aged so?"

Lilian shook her head. "Did you lock the door, Mae?"

"I always do, why?"

"Because I can hear him. And he's thinking about when he escaped from Broadmoor, when he made a key for a lock and got out."

Mae searched Lilian's face, which was far-away with the blood-sight. "The asylum? When was he at Broadmoor?" she asked in fascination.

"After he killed his wife," whispered Lilian.

"Forget it, who cares?" said Mae. "You fed, he's gone, we're sleeping, that's it. What's wrong with you?"

Lilian flashed around, stricken, grabbing Mae by the shoulders. "He's thinking about another woman he did in, in New York, Mae. And all the others in London. No one's ever caught him. And now he's thinking about how to kill us."

Mae scoffed. "He's a *man*, Lil."

"He's standing at the back door, waiting."

Mae actually got a chill then, all the way through her non-beating heart. "Why?"

"Waiting for us to sleep."

"Then what?"

A long moment passed, Lilian's eyes searching nothingness as she listened.

"Then he's getting a mirror, and coming back for us," she said finally.

A mirror. To bend the sun around corners. Oh, *God*. Mae flew to the room door and peered through the keyhole. It was already too light to go anywhere, the tepid dawn was already on the floorboards.

"How long 'til the drug makes him forget? Lil? Lil?"

Mae turned back, but Lilian was already asleep, the somnolent drive having taken her. Mae backed away from the door, imagining she could hear a blade being sharpened, a key turning, the hiss of fire.

Too late, she was asleep.

Too late for the footstep on the cobbles.

Too late to see the man's face, a grim smile.

Too late.

Jack was back.

THE EDGE

Night is coming; it is time to fight.

I try to hold still while ten nymphs weave steel wire into my sneakers, but I'm cross-legged on the floorboards and getting a cramp. I shift, and fairies hauling arrow buckets whisper past my ear, their wings spilling rainbows on a ring of textbooks and Milo-crusted cups. All day, the Folk have turned my pages and tested me, as they did when I went to school in the city. But much has changed. I'm older, on a college study break, and this farmhouse is not the city, not yet. Once, it was an island in miles of scrub. But the suburbs grew right to the doorstep, and the Folk came with the sprawl. Now, while one side of the farmhouse hears traffic in the distance; the other faces the scrub, the billabong, the cool valley air …

… and the reason for this armor.

A green man barks orders to the sprites and dwarves, his leafy arms a-dance. Tommyknockers poke the floorboards, thinking of tunnels and going underground. A gnome stands on an upturned basket and tugs a breast-plate across my chest. He ties on old boot laces to make it fit, then frowns at a standard, teacup-sized gnome helm. He throws it back and casts appraisal at the laundry bucket. I give him a stare, mouthing *no*. I'm not doing the Ned Kelly thing. But his face is lined with fear, something I've never seen.

I relent and accept the spear the gnome pushes into my hand. I put my thumb in the middle, thinking I could break it in half. My Gran—well, everyone's Gran—says the Folk are what makes us people; that they are magic in the mundane, that we need them to survive. And sometimes, they need us too. Folk battles are nothing new but they tell me this is different. They're at war with something bigger. Something they never met in Europe. Things that lived before there was Europe at all.

The creatures.

The gnome raps my arm and I stretch. The Folk fill the living room, a carpet of crawling color, formed in lines and battle-dressed. Sprites in phoenix feathers, borrowers in patchwork shirts. The green man shuffles down the assembled ranks.

I stay out of it. This is Folk war and I know my role. I'm their lookout tower, and a platform for the fairy archers, nothing more. The gnome hands the platform over: my mother's old brown kitchen tray. He must have rumbled past a good deal of Tupperware to get to that.

The sun dips and the green man commands us outside. The tommyknockers crack a mini-bar rum bottle and scoop handfuls of Dutch-courage. I pretend not to notice, but the smell pulls memories of a boozy college party: drunken pranks and hallucinations. I'm tired; I want this over so I can sleep, and get this laundry bucket off my head.

We face the disputed territory. Beyond the pavers, where the Sir Walter lawn fades into native violets, is the half-full billabong, its water like a shard of dark glass against the hill. And this is the problem. It hasn't rained in a long while, and the creatures guard the water. Water for blooming hanging pots, for Folk herbs, for the gardens. The dam is deep, but the creatures don't want to share.

So we wait, as dusk fades the sky to indigo. The Folk fan out beneath me: fine-boned gnomes, shifting sprites, old green men and foil-armored dwarves. Tinny armor clinks. Crickets chirp, a deafening chant.

Then, they stop.

The lake appears to sink, gathering weight, and the hackles stand on my neck. For the first time, my heart pounds.

Then, they come.

The creatures rise as shape and shadow, slinking from the water. Some are dark bulks, while others twist like snakes. They shimmer across the horizon, camouflaged for twilight. The Folk gasp collective. I recoil; they are *big*. I want to run inside to the fireplace, to hot chocolate and crash notes.

But it's too late.

A green man cries the battle forward. My kitchen tray bounces as the fairies launch, loosing arrows like confetti. The tommyknockers stream across the pavers and dig. But the creatures are already on them.

A bulking water shadow at the turf edge swipes a fat plug of air, catching two fairies in an eddy. They crash into the violets, and a twisting snake consumes them. The gnomes and sprites thrust spears at the bulking shadow, but it rolls like a liquid balloon, leaving mud and water. The Folk slide into a gathered pool and drown in the slick.

Tears choke me; I have never seen Folk die before. They fall like insects, easily snuffed. I'm to stay out of it, but I want to run and pull them out. The fairies regroup on the tray. Then I see a snake shadow curling around the green men's left flank.

I call a warning, but too late. The snake rears and hisses with a desiccating breath. It sucks my eyeballs dry, and the green men's bodies wither, falling in piles of autumnal red. My chest is a pressure pain that demands hurt repaid. I grab a deck chair. The tommyknockers surface under the snake, but they won't make it.

The snake rears. I shove the fairy tray on the chair and swing a rake at the water creature's head. I hear angry shouts from a green man: I've gone beyond the front line; all defenses are behind. A snake whips black around my feet. The native violets crunch under my hip, and then all I hear is rustling. The ground whips past as the creatures drag me to the water. Then I smash my head on a rocky crop and the stars go dancing: overhead in the sky and underneath in the still water surface.

I wake in the cold and dark. At first, I think I've left a window open. Then I find damp soil instead of a mattress.

I can't rise. A fleshy weight presses my legs. Dark eyes hover over mine, and beyond, I see an arched neck. The shadow snake is coiled about my thighs, my jeans wet underneath.

"Lay still," says the snake between tiny, threatening breaths. My muscles clamp against my will. The water creatures creep in, murky depths and obsidian edges. I smell the stink of still water.

"Why do you help them?" rumbles a different voice, as if the Earth has spoken.

"Yes. Why?" repeats the snake.

The question wrenches at my chest and puts rocks in my throat. It takes my mind to the edge of some abyss. I see the weeping willow silhouette the full moon, and below, the moon and tree repeated in the dam surface. The edge between blurs; I clutch my head, spinning, spinning.

"Is it not enough you bring them here?" The snake, again.

"Who?" I croak, losing the abyss. I am dreaming, perhaps. Just dreaming.

"White fellas like you, the small ones, the savages." *The Folk.*

"They need water and you kill them, of course they fight back!" I think I shout. But the blood feeding my consciousness is thin and angry. I want to tell them that the Folk are older than humanity, that they watch our lives and dreams. That they only fight for water; water these creatures could share.

The snake's lidless eyes catch the edge of dawn, as if the night has disappeared. The water beings become lenses bending time and light: red, orange, yellow and green shimmers. I feel as if hours have passed, perhaps decades. I panic.

"Let me go," I plead.

The snake slides away and my body responds again. I scramble to run, but I stop: my jeans are red with blood. I stare as the wounded snake coils herself into a dam-edge puddle, shimmering like an oil film.

"You don't see," says the snake. "You fellas sink your roots shallow and live with your bad dreams …"

The snake points its tail at me, rattling like dry bones. "… now you'll see." The words melt with the reed-whispering wind, and could have been nothing more. The water creatures sink, receding before the sun. The tendrils of night dissolve into nothingness. I'm lying by the lake, its surface still, a wad of al-foil and bootlaces bunched in one armpit.

This feels like the end of a bender. My head certainly hurts. I rub a tender spot at the crown, then pat down my jeans. They're wet and muddy. I could have just fallen in the dewy grass. I run to the house without looking back.

The Folk are euphoric, having thought me lost. But I stalk around the farmhouse, unsettled. The rooms are spick and clean, but I smell rum. The past night sinks into the weirdness between dreams and memory repressed. The house is too bright, the hour too early. I close my door on the Folk and fall on the covers.

It's afternoon when I get up, bad tempered and sore. The Folk flock to my door, eager to share in my story, but I'm not in the mood and push them away. They scatter, but then hang at the edges of vision, glancing, observing, and for the first time, that makes me mad.

I want to be alone. I pace around the kitchen. If there'd been mess, I'd have cleaned to get my mind off things, but the Folk have done it all. I look at my study books, still strewn on the rug. I smell rum again, stale and lingering. It turns my stomach, so I go outside. The Folk don't follow, now. Hanging baskets sway gently from the roof beams. One plant has dropped a runner into the turf. Its row of glossy green leaves makes a track through the native violets, spoiling the mat of purple nodding heads. I see another runner, and another. They crisscross the violets, erasing the crisp edge; I follow them past the shade and into the sun where, finally, the silver grasses take over.

This bothers me. I stalk around the house. Across the road, an estate fence runs unbroken into the distance. The urban edge.

I twitch my shoulders, wanting space. And that's when I go towards the billabong lake.

In the scrub, relief replaces anger. I cover the hundred yards in grass-swished steps. In the light, the dam surface is a mirror reflecting the sky. No sign of creatures. I pause at the willow-licked edge, then climb the hill beyond. My socks gather spear-grass and the sun beats until my breaths are heavy. I flop down on the rocky ridge and take off my boots.

When I was five, Dad worked away and we lived at the farmhouse. I would come up here just to see the vast horizon, and imagine he wasn't far away. Then, the farmhouse stuck out of naked scrub that rolled in every direction. Now, it's a pock abutting a sea of tin roofs. And I notice other things now: shaggy hedges escaping from the estate, cane toads rustling in the dam reeds, the smell of Lantana in the air.

I snatch at the spear-grass. The barbs tear tufts of sock-flesh, and released, float inland, away from the suburbs. My mood sours. The distant city seems a great fungus, feeding, growing. I feel a foreigner for the first time.

I turn and stare the other way. The land curves into a basin, holding a cluster of snowy-trunked gums. Muted colors: gray-greens, dusky pinks and ochre. That's how I can see the stuff that doesn't belong. The lime head of prickly-pear, the bright leaves of a Chinese elm. I push my eyes with the heels of my hands. The world is tilting over and leaving me behind.

Finally, I lie back and stare at the sky. Sometime, after the lorikeets go shrieking overhead, I close my eyes.

I dream it is night again, and the land is formed of creatures. They are silent as they move, both time and substance. They are rock tumbles become waterfalls, regathering as still pools. They rise from the billabong, larger than the sky, muddy water coursing with serpentine rainbows. Closing.

A twitter snaps my eyes open. An Indian mynah skips by. It twists a sleek head, brown and orange, and a word drops onto my tongue.

Invader.

I scramble up. It cocks its head, then darts into the scrub. Unafraid. Here to stay. And something unfinished inside my head completes. The sun is already down, and the night air creeps up the hill, promising danger. The lake is a dark hole, and I know the creatures are rising again.

I stumble down the rocks, wanting to be home. There's a light on in the farmhouse. But back on the low ground, the estate lights align and I lose the path. For a few seconds, the world spins—

lights, dark, lights—then, a splash.

I run blind. The lights bob and silver grass whips around my feet like hands trying to pull me down. I pump my arms and pray for pavers. Finally, I see color: the hanging baskets, and the farmhouse—roof, veranda and door.

Color. Everywhere.

A qualm bursts through my consciousness.

I hit the brakes still within the violets, and ease my foot back from the pavers. The Folk line the patio edge. And the gutters. And the roof. Thousands upon thousands, a swarm. The silver grass winds around my ankles. But it's not a snare, now. More like a hand that saves you from a fall.

Tommyknocker vibrations course through my feet. The green men and the sprites are a heaving ground cover. The air moves as they inhale and exhale as one, Folk with no edge at all. Their posture says I am not welcome; I am not what left this morning. That I know secrets no one should know.

Behind me, the creatures rise with the full moon. Just enough light to see the nightmares I know I've seen and forgotten: the Folk's razor teeth and cruel black eyes. Their ears cut to points, their battle-scars, their cruel smiles. They are opportunists, magic weavers, manipulators, and make glamour to hide it all. They look into my heart and they know I have seen. If I was a child they would trick me and I would forget. Or if I didn't, they would change me for another. But I am grown now. I've seen.

I can never live among Folk again

I am in no man's land between them and the creatures. I want to dissociate, to castle like a rook. But I can't claim neutrality. The Folk are ours, we brought them here.

I have a vision then: a hard, future-reel that knocks me to my knees. The tommyknockers will break through the violets. The Folk will drag me down under the turf, or, in pieces, into their hiding places in the walls. They will feed me to the Lantana spilling out into the scrub. And they will push the creatures back and back, until the advancing edge reaches the end of land and there is only legend left.

There is nowhere to go. I don't belong in this country, the land of the creatures. But they are the ones holding against invasion.

I pick up a tree branch, hard and gnarled.
Night is coming. It is time to fight.

PARVAZ

S ome days, when the alley streamers snap in the breeze, and I smell the upper atmosphere come down to mingle in the detritus of these shops and stones, I sit in this chair and fester an evil longing for what can never be again. My shoulder aches where the bone healed amiss, the wasted muscles clamped. Remembering my body stuffed into this human form, my treasures broken down and sold. And the one who both saved me and chained me.

The bells ring from the shop door. A woman is there, framed in the doorway. A shock of ebony hair, a silhouette of arms and hips.

And desire stirs, low down in my brain.

She approaches tentatively, as if she smells something that makes her nervous, as if it is too dark for her to see. She moves like a hunted thing, making my spine tingle and my leg muscles burn.

I rise, silent, and watch her from this doorway. Her fingers moving to the glass case nearest, her eyes flickering to the side, lingering on the jewels. She has the sway of a princess. She wears loose culottes like a veiled dancer. An exotic thing that lived in the palace, perhaps, when I lived in the mountains long ago. My desire unfolds until my mouth is dry, my neck sore from the clench of hunting muscles, but I won't allow more. Above her shimmering pants is just a T-shirt, her features too light for a sultana. Besides, there would be questions, and I need her to pay.

I show myself, and she jumps a fraction, which sets my heart racing, pupils expanding, the shop with its cases and old wood and silken drapes suddenly blooming in spectrum shift. The detail floods my consciousness: a mouse lurks in the far corner, thinking himself unseen; beetle bodies on the door lintel, their rainbow shells dull; dust and wood polish and earthly things. Cloying. And my plodding, human brain tries to give it all meaning.

I'm overcome and stagger, strike my knee. Pain sends the human brain away and brings me clear. The woman rushes over. I smell her relief, and her perfume; she sees an old man, a weak man. She has dismissed what scared her only moments ago. But I am neither old, nor weak, nor a man, and she smells familiar … of blood and feathers.

She helps me aloft the floor. "Goodness, are you alright?" she asks. "Do you want me to—"

Just a small stumble, a slip! I protest, allowing my hand to linger on her proffered arm. My own skin feels strange, but her form underneath it familiar. Bones in meat.

"You have beautiful things," she says, allowing the moment to pass. She moves to the cabinets. I slip into the counter and shadow her interest.

She stops by the middle case. "These here." She traces the outlines. My gaze is steady even as my heart is twisting in my human chest, seeing what she is seeing. These are brooches, all wings. Wings half-furled, wings in glide … and below them, feathers in silver and gold and platinum. All my treasures remade.

She sighs. "Birds," she says, as if this conveys something. I say nothing. So many customers begin this way.

"I love birds," she continues. "Such freedom. I'm sure I'd love to be able to fly. To be so carefree. Is that why you make these?"

Her gesture indicates the shop. She already knew of this place, perhaps. From a friend, or by reputation. The odd jeweler down the little side alley in this big, ugly city, where every piece is a wing or feather, or a beak. But she is mistaken—of my reasons, and what she sees. *No,* I say, but softly, and she pays me no attention.

I hope that she will pick quickly, but she lingers as they always do. I rub my shoulder, and look out the window. She moves across the shop, but I still smell the feathers on her skin.

"I have a bird," she says softly, when the silence becomes uncomfortable for her.

Ah, I say, though I mean it explains how she smells and not because I am interested. She is waiting now for me to ask what sort of bird it is, but I do not care. Instead, I ask what she is looking for.

"Something," she says vaguely, browsing distractedly, until she looks in the cases opposite. Her turned back brings me a memory, though it should not. A cave, and that smell of blood and feathers. I have been too long in this body, and yet I can never leave.

When I look up again, she is gone. The door is closing with its cheerful chime. I turn the latch and flip over the sign. *Parvaz* is closed for now.

I numb the human in me with spirits and perch on an old chair to go over my books. My savior—my jailer—is due his fee. There is enough for this time, but not yet for the next. I glower at the closed shop with its cases, its propensity to attract customers. Its position beneath the perfect and unattainable sky.

Two weeks pass and I sell only a little. The customers like the jewels; they come to the shop from the tent markets outside, happy and pleasant; but they do not like me. My mood matters, and I work on improving it, like the helpless living thing I am. That desire to live is what got me here. I spend half a day mulling on this, then I improve.

I am surprised and annoyed when she comes back. The girl with the ebony hair and the preyish ways. I rub my shoulder, wondering if she could know my thoughts. She hovers in the doorway while I stare. She looks different, though I know it is her. She has changed her hair, perhaps.

"Hello again," she says. Advances two tentative steps.

You were here before, I manage. I stand behind the counter, feeling my human self all thin and fragile. As if I could crack my skin like an eggshell and emerge again. I fix on her, then realize I am not blinking. I have to remember to do that. I do it twice. Slowly. She seems to settle.

"Do you make custom pieces?" she asks. She blinks, too. Her eyes are very green. The flesh around them is soft. My hands clench against the wood. It takes a long moment to recover. I apologize and lie: ask her to repeat herself. I am not sure what she has said.

She does, but as I form the word *no*, two thoughts clash together. The first is that this is a sale. The second is how little money I have for the djinni.

And what he will do to me if I cannot pay.

So I nod. She smiles, a tiny movement at the edge of her lips. She is nervous again; she feels exposed. I see the pulse at her neck and wrists. I wish she would leave.

Do you know what you want? I ask. I rub my jaw with the back of my arm, and it feels odd. Smooth where there should be feathers.

She is already turning to go. "I will do a sketch and come back?"

Relieved at the distance, I nod. She is gone again. The smell does not linger long, but my shoulder is itching now.

I go to the back room and pace about my chair, scratching. My eyes fall absently on the ledger. I strain my good shoulder, searching my back with my paltry nails. I find a lump.

I seek the tiny relief room with its mirror. I undo the buttons and pull my shirt away. The scar wraps my arm like a strangling snake. I pull the wasted arm forward. Something is there, its tip protruding through my skin. I think of burrs, or parasites.

I snatch the fine pliers from my workbench and close them about this thing. I tug. It comes loose with a sting I've known before, and I thrust the offending object up to the light. A white feather, a bloody quill. I lose my grip and the pliers fall. The feather floats to the pale porcelain sink, where it sticks, fanned and wetted. I hold myself, shivering, as the blood creeps pinkly into drops.

She comes back in two days with a white sheet folded in her hands. She looks different again, hair piled high on her head, her neck exposed. I try not to look further, but retreat into my human brain, the one that thinks of how to handle tools and work metals, and not about how to hunt, or how to rip out a slender throat.

She unfolds the sheet and pushes it across. I look down and the picture shudders in my vision. *No, no! I cannot make this!*

She sees my expression. "I'm sorry, the drawing isn't very good," she stumbles. "It's a necklace, you see?"

I do. I see the curve of the band intended to grace her neck, and erupting from the side of it, the motif she would have me create. The rendering is so good, it could fly off her page.

I cannot make this, I say, pushing the paper back towards her. I hope to convey that I have not the skill for such a design, though I do. But this thing is too large, and renders an image the djinni forbade me to make.

Her big eyes are sad. "Oh please!" she begs. "You're perfect for it. No one else can make it!" She gestures around the shop, as if to remind me that I make wings and beaks and talons already. But never a form complete. Never that. The djinni would have me.

"How much do you need?" she says quickly. And this is the critical moment. I have not sold enough this month. The djinni can have me anyway if I cannot pay. I stand there, in dithering silence, my fingers moving like inch-worms against the glass. I tell myself I can stop work before the size is too large, that I can tell her I cannot do it later. I will sell other things to make the payment, and destroy this piece without finishing it.

She raises her eyebrows, hopeful. I look away. I name a hideous price, more than enough to pay the djinni for a half-year.

She nods slowly. "I will pay you half now?" she asks. Her hand darts to her bag. So swift. So unexpected. I catch her before I realize what I have done. She stares at me, frightened green eyes, my hand closed about her wrist.

No, no, I say, dropping her. In my head, my tongue is tasting her blood. *Pay when I finish*. For then there is no transgression until the end.

She almost protests, but I have scared her. She leaves me with the drawing and the rising panic in my ill-fitting body prison. I go to walk into the back, but a fit comes and I throw the paper down. My head is full of her design: a bird, wings outstretched, a hunting form, talons out, eyes focused. I felt that, once. I shrug off the human brain, and the smell of prey sharpens. I leap onto the cabinets and scan the revealed shadows. The mouse is still there, I sense him. I wait, watching him along his usual track. I pounce.

The cabinet crashes to the side. I'm aware of the mouse-steps, accelerating. But this body is ungainly. My good shoulder crashes into the wall. A silk drape comes down. I chase the small gray haunches and lose the ability to recall.

When I wake later, it is dark and I am under a cabinet. The shop is a mess. There is fur on my lips and blood in my mouth. Even after I have cleaned, I am not sure if it is mine or mouse.

I work on the piece in a feverish state. For the first two days, my hand shakes whenever I think of it, and I cannot begin any part of the bird. I raid my treasures and make the circlet from a platinum sword pommel. I select diamonds for inlay from a sultana's bracelet, and gold and silver from other jewels that once sparkled in the mountain sun.

She comes back in two days. I show her the circlet, and she leaves quickly. I stare after her again, trying to place how she looks different each time. Maybe just because I have been dreaming of her blood and flesh.

I make the parts for the bird over the next three days, but I do not meld them. Each is small enough not to exceed the djinni's conditions, but even still, I begin to dream of the night I hunted, and woke up in the djinni's palace, a slave for eternity.

The next time the woman returns, I refuse to show her my work. *I am not happy with it*, I say. *Besides, my tooth is hurting and it gives me a headache.* She purses her lips. She tries to persuade me. She is excited to see her piece, she reassures me she will love it. I refuse more sternly. I tell her to come back later, that I am not feeling well.

After she leaves I stare at the pieces on my bench, holding the tooth through my pallid cheek. Sales are still not enough to meet my payment. But I am scared of this piece, of making a whole picture. My human mind is strong on craft and finances, but it has limits in regulating my real self. If I make this thing, will my mind break? Will I hunt this woman and kill her? Will I be found, imprisoned and unable to pay the djinni?

My fingers slip inside my lips to test the tooth. I grunt, surprised, as it comes away in my hand. My focus shifts to the twisted roots, pinkly stained. Am I hallucinating?

I lie on my cot and push the tooth back into place. It fits with a dull pain, and later when I wake, it sits solid in my gum.

My hand sweeps the work pieces into a box and shoves them beneath the cot. Then I dream of the mountain air, of wings so large they spanned the peaks, a cave of treasures, and a dozen other things gone forever. And I wake with my shoulder aching and tears on my cheeks.

She returns again in two days, in a suit this time, her hair braided tightly behind her head. She smiles again. "How long to go now?" she asks. "Can I pay you?"

I don't respond, but this time I take her to the workbench. I have taken the pieces from the box, unchanged. I have prepared this moment. I tell her I cannot complete the piece, but that she can take the pieces to someone else to assemble. I have not been well, I say. I show her my hand. It shakes with the restless nights and the fear of being imprisoned. But if she will buy the pieces separate, I can pay the djinni; another month will go on.

She purses her lips, but she puts a kind hand to my shoulder. "But I want you to finish it. You must."

I stare at the platinum wing, at the exquisite detail on the feathers. No wonder she does not believe I cannot complete it. But I wish she would not touch me, those blood-smelling fingers on my wasted flesh. I step away.

"Do you know what this is?" she says softly, tapping her finger on the now-smudged drawing. "I looked up the name of your shop," she continues, as if this will explain it. "*Parvaz*. Persian. And so"—she taps the drawing—"is this *rukh*. So, you have to finish it. Please. No one else can. I have your money all ready."

I stand a long moment, my true name tripping ugly memories, knowing I have no time to make other sales. My shoulder aches. I dare not look at her.

Friday, I say. *Come back Friday.*

When she is gone, I open the shop windows, and the door. Outside, the market tents crowd together under the building walls and sky. The breeze snaps pennants at the tent crowns, the air cool. I look for ebony hair. There is none, but I am bothered the same.

I make a wheeling turn back into the shop. The breeze is lofting the silk drapes, like it did in a sultan's palace, long ago. I stop in the entrance to the back room, see the pieces lying on their table.

She said *Persian* … unusual. And she said *rukh*, not roc. Perhaps she is a scholar? But her keenness to pay … I rub at my shoulder. The ache is dull now, as usual. I stand there and ponder, as the sun goes down and evening comes.

Then, I go to my workbench, take up the pieces, both those in gold and the ones in my head. And I smell jasmine coming in from the street.

I am dreaming again, though this is a place I have been before. Another cave in my mountains, but one lower down, reachable for a great bird with a broken wing. I am frantic in the way living things are when they are going to die and can't accept it. I know who lives here and should not go in; this djinni is clever; he knows how to trap things, even one as great as I.

I should not go, but I want to live. I need the djinni's magic. For how can a rukh hunt with this useless wing? A piece of feather drifts to the djinni's feet. He seems a savior. He can make me a human body, where a wing is not essential. But I must pay him each moon, in human money, not with my treasures. And those I cannot sell as they are; they must be transformed, but never as a bird-form complete, or weighing more than my broken feather. He twirls the white shape in his hand. I will starve slowly, or take this chance.

I work through the remaining days and Friday comes with the piece finished on my bench. It violates every term of my salvation. Too large; showing a bird-form complete. In those last hours, its emerging splendor sent me mad with memory. Snowmelt I could taste, clear skies I could see. But now it is done.

My shoulder aches. It should. She is nearly here. I have put this puzzle together. My heart bounds for what could happen now.

The bells chime on the door, and she enters. Again, different. Sharper, less feminine. I show myself.

She smiles, again, a quick movement. My reflexes scream, but I control them now. I am focused.

I am hunting.

"You are finished?" she asks.

I nod and beckon her towards the workroom. She comes almost reluctantly. I shift my shoulders against the prickle there, like feathers pushing against a cloth. A feeling that now makes sense. She pauses in the door as she sees the finished piece.

Her *rukh* streams in gold, platinum and jewels, immaculate. She grasps it in her hands, testing the weight.

"I should pay you," she says.

This, here, is the moment. I look her in the eye as she hands across the cash. The contract closes. And then, for a second, I see the flames dance in her pupils. As soon as I take the notes, her smile twists, and I have confirmation of who she is.

"You are mine, *rukh*," she says. She does not bother to disguise her voice now. It is the rumble of the djinni. My mind gives me pictures of dungeons in his mountain palace. The djinni bounces the piece in her hand. "Too heavy for our contract," she says. "And a form complete, besides."

I am not blinking now. I am fixed, waiting for what she will do. My back itches, my shoulder burns. Wait.

"You will be my slave now," she says, slipping the piece about her neck, satisfied. My blood thrums as I see her pulse there, just against the circlet. "I have waited a long time, *rukh*, to have you like this."

You tricked me, I say. *You asked me to do this!*

She laughs, not unkindly. "There is no rule against that. Now come."

My vision focuses on that one square inch of flesh. *But you have broken a rule too*, I say. You were too confident. You forgot something.

She laughs, amused. Her pulse rises and falls. "And what is that?"

I can hurt you.

She laughs again. "You are trapped in that form, *rukh*, and I am immortal. You cannot hurt me."

My smile, if I could, would be slow. She has not realized what I have, why I felt as I did each time she came. *Your magic does not work when you wear human form.*

Then the feathers rip through my skin, the talons burst my

shoes.

But my beak is what kills her. It plunges into that soft neck and spills blood and flesh across the floor. I feast on her lifeless form, hunted and destroyed. And it tastes like winging over imaginary mountains, like freedom I once had.

THE ONE YOU FEED

Sometimes, betrayals are innocuous things. Your friend tells your secret when they promised not. You hate them for it, but real damage is slight, so the elders say. No one takes slights of word seriously here, where a boy is born with two selves. When every day until the age of fifteen is focused on refining the good-self and shunning the monstrous self, until that day, at rite of passage, when the boy enters the stadium and slays his dark self so the good will become the adult.

For Garrick, that day is today.

I am nervous. Garrick's twin-self crosses the red dust, far beneath the rising seats. A sheer wall separates him from the watchers, and above is a ring of archers. He enters a twin, two boys the same, but only one will leave. And if the monster is the victor, then none will. I could lose this friend today.

But no one thinks the worst will happen; it almost never does. Boys are trained in how to protect their good selves, how to nurture them with learning. Their fathers pass the wisdom of their own battles; those with fathers, at least. I finger the stones behind my back, wondering if I can still feel regret about that. I wait, but none comes. No, then. I am cured of it.

Garrick, both of him, makes his bows. No one can tell which is the good-self and which is the monster; that will come only with victory. But I can tell. I know him well.

They each take an edged weapon from their belts, and step

away into the dust, as if they are just to spar. Expectation is oddly dim here; the crowd almost look bored. Good, that is good. They think they know Garrick well. They know he is the son of the highest elder, the most educated, the most dedicated. Destined for greatness. This is almost a formality; his monstrous self should be so weak from neglect, the battle will be over quickly.

The first blows fall metal on metal. Good-Garrick and monster-Garrick circle and clash. Dust rises, cloaking their skin, sticking to sweat. They are soon both red-dust boys, no skin to be seen, and only the metal edges glint through the fray. Then, there is a stumble. One Garrick goes down, the crowd leans forward. The other Garrick does not hesitate; he drives the point of the blade through the downed Garrick's chest. The downed Garrick jerks around the blade, curled like a spider on its back, then flops still.

My heart fights my breath for space in my throat. My skin drums with the noise from the stands. The victor Garrick stands before the applause, a red-skinned version of the Garrick who walked in. He closes his eyes and raises his palms, salute to the elders. The archers relax. Then, Garrick retrieves his sword and strides towards the exit.

No elder moves. They maintain applause, standing now, tears on some faces. Pride, I believe, for they see the good-Garrick leave. Passed through the rite, and now to be a man. This is the great moment for them.

For them.

I do not stay to witness more but descend to the arena level on the seldom-used stair. Garrick is waiting in the tunnel, and he brings his eyes up from the dust. We look at each other, with our black irises reflecting the torchlight. Garrick, so dusty no one can see the evil marks. Me, with the control I learned from my father, using my mind to not show the marks. Monsters, both.

This is the great moment.

I offer the eye lenses he will need to stay concealed. Garrick nods his thanks. He has learned well in all our lessons, proved himself capable of skill and concealment, even from his good-self. And the good-self never realized another could teach his monster just as well. My pride burns my eyes when he leaves.

Now good-Garrick lies dead in the dust. The elders will be

slack, not bothering to clean the body of the assumed monster-self. They will not find the unmarred skin.

You see, some betrayals are innocuous, but others are not. Words can cut as deep as a sword, and bring death when spoken wrong. The good-Garrick told my secret and so now the monster has his chance.

THE 7:40 FROM PARABURDOO

D ave fumbles for the jack and splits a nail against its metal. The tearing pain brings curses, words that fall dead at his feet. He bites his lip to silence, exposed under the word-eating, indigo sky. His body tenses like an animal. He darts his gaze from the ribbon road to the scrappy grass tussocks, then further to the low hills, barely standing out from the pre-dawn sky. He sucks the finger and the blood taste spirals his thoughts, down to the black earth under all that grass. He comes apart, scattering like spilled crazy balls. *There's something out there, he thinks, looking back from beyond the headlights.* That hunts; that eats. That sees this lame Prado, obvious speck in the lonely Pilbara road.

Hurry.

He gets his mind back, hefts the jack and slams the rear door. His words won't echo, but this bang does. Sound rejected, not of interest. Dave thinks, *the land knows what to listen for.* It knows his voice. Will hunt him. Erase him. Knows he's stopped, vulnerable. Full on crazy stuff. Gives him the creeps. Air gusts, lifts his shirt, but nothing else moves. He shivers. Dave left Mt Tom Price two hours ago. Wishes he'd done it sooner. The mine's there, the mine where he worked. He's supposed to be on shift now.

He's still forty clicks from the airstrip in Paraburdoo, where the seven-forty to Perth will get him out. Forty long k's through the twisting Pilbara road. He glances at his bare wrist; watch missing, forgotten.

Doesn't matter, keep moving.

He snatches up the nut shifter, bangs his knee on the tow bar as he hurries round to the busted tire. He feels for the wheel nuts, covered in fine red dust. His cargos and boots are thick with the stuff; it's in his hair and nostrils, parching him dry as roo bones cracking in the Pilbara sun.

He hears faint rushing; a truck maybe, somewhere near the horizon. He stands, straining to hear, his mind gone animal again. The sound bounces and comes at him from all around. He thinks, *the road winds on itself, I'll drive and drive and get nowhere at all.*

He works faster, wrestling with panic. He knows the road. He counts the bends to Paraburdoo in his head. Ordered thought. Banish what has happened. But he checks the silence after each nut. He wants sound – a car, a birdcall, anything – and yet he doesn't want them. Alone is safer. But then he listens until the silence becomes creepy. And he starts to think like he's a child again, when monsters hid in shadows, and he felt their breath on his shoulder, and the worst thing was when the silence was broken. He starts with the tire again. Nut, dust, metal, dust. Thoughts come unbidden now. He remembers where this started.

There was an accident. A bad one. Well, *incident*, said the paperwork. Three men in the crusher, red stains among the red dust. Just a terrible accident. But Dave knew better. He was meant to be in there too; he'd been on that shift. The three guys had been his mates. But Dave knew the crusher wasn't at fault; no, that wasn't it. All this was because of the black ore.

Dave has the last nut in his hand when he remembers the jack, still sitting on the road. He's forgotten it, like his watch and jacket. Got the tire nearly undone and everything. Frustration strips a curse from his throat. He's scared for real. Been stopped too long. Needs to get moving. His voice shakes as he talks to himself. He wants to stop, but he can't, he's getting crazy. He drags the jack into place, fumbles along the chassis for the spot.

A footstep clicks on the asphalt. Dave whirls, flashlight in his teeth, and drool slicks cold around to his chin. He snatches the thing from his teeth. The thin beam shakes as he lights up the tar. A man stands on the road, just feet in the torchbeam, straddling the dashed white line. Boots with odd laces, odd socks. Feet pointed his way, shins angled because he's leaning forward. Watching him. *Johnno.* Dave swings the light up to the face, but Johnno is gone. There's nothing on the road, just the meaty lump of a dead roo.

Of course. Johnno is dead like the others. Dave tells himself he's seeing things, but he doesn't quite believe it. This cold sweat is a truth serum, tells him his fears are real. That if he doesn't get his ass on that plane and off this soil, he'll be dead meat too. There's a slickness in his palms, blood or oil, or both mixing with the dust. It doesn't matter. It can't matter. He spins the jack up, faster and faster.

He'd been doing the same thing when he'd first heard about the black ore. One of the haul trucks had blown a hose out on the pit road. He'd been in the crib room, got the call to come down and get the thing moving again. Tons were what counted. So he'd taken a ute and got out there. Twenty minutes later, up to his elbows in red-dirt laden grease, Troy had crackled on the radio.

"How much longer, Dave?"

"Nearly done."

"Good. You hear about pit four?"

"What about it?"

"New ore type. Geo's excited."

Dave grunted. Didn't take much to excite guys who were into rocks. This was the Pilbara. Rocks every-bloody-where. "So what?"

Troy's voice rung with excitement. "You'll see, Dave." Then the radio had crackled on the sign off, like laughter of the mad. And Dave had cut his hand on the hydraulic line.

Later, Dave had seen the black ore. Touched it with his bleeding hand. It was sticky like pitch and shot with iron-loaded red, nothing like the yellow clay stuff coming out of the other pits. The Geos sampled it with their gloved hands, but standing by the sample pile, Dave and his crew had crumbled it in their fingers. It was odd stuff. Soft like graphite, until you squeezed, and then it would harden, like a fist of ball-bearings. And it infected him with unease. He began to think of arguments he'd had: union meetings, old girlfriends, guys he'd picked fights with when he was juiced. And these wrongs ran into something deeper, beyond himself, as if the ore was after a payback, come to collect something he could give.

The loader operator hadn't touched it, but he crossed himself and didn't turn up next shift. The super cursed the superstition, but Dave envied the guy. He'd had it right. He knew a bad thing when he saw it. But by then, too late. The haul trucks had dumped two hundred tons of it into the ROM hopper, and the black ore went down to the crushers.

Dave has the wasted tire off now. He shoves it towards the road shoulder where it crunches down the hill. It vanishes amongst the silvery grass and topples, leaving a black mass in a silver sea.

He regrets that. Black mass in the grass, black like the ore. It looks like the pictures in his head now, the ones he's had since he touched the stuff. Of black shapes lying silent in the town streets, in their car seats, by the road like roos … silent because they were dead.

The black ore had gone down into the crusher, and like rocks could bleed, it broke open with splashes of oily black and ruby red. *Land blood*, Dave had thought. Something that should not have been dug up. Something come to claim a price.

The crusher jammed. And control was on the radio.

"Fault in the belt and the number two screen. Check it out."

Dave's team was meant to go in there, the usual crew: him, Johnno, Troy, Casper and Rob, the apprentice. Dave and Casper had cut the power and locked the crusher out, done the clear and trial. The lights on the switch had gone out; Dave had seen it, Casper'd checked it. Then Dave had watched Casper push the start, and the crusher'd sat, quiet and dark and jammed with the black ore. Power confirmed off. Clear to go.

The radio had crackled; another downed haul truck on the pit road and no one else available. Dave was called away. So Johnno, Troy and Rob had gone in with the breaker bars. And Casper had stood, a silent and surly sentry, as Dave had been going down the stairs.

That was when the crusher started. Dave had flown back up the stairs, following the black chute of unearthly screams. The crusher door was locked, fused around its seams; they couldn't get in. Casper had yelled over the din until his voice broke, the radio crackled that there wasn't any power, and what the hell? Dave had staggered. Nothing to do but reel. The crusher had eaten his boys alive.

Dave grips the new tire tight, ready to throw it if he needs to. His own feet crunching on the gravel is too much now; he holds himself rigid. But silence too eats at sanity. He must get on. He can't miss the flight.

He feels for the bolt shanks, pinches another finger between the new tire and the wheel arch. By now, his fingers are painful stubs. He fumbles for the nuts. One, two … three are enough. Three. Three men in the crusher. Terror chases his hands. He tries not to think about Casper. But he sees him in his head sometimes. Along with the other dark, dead bodies. The ones that start to move again.

Casper was meant to be on the next night shift, but he hadn't come. Dave got the call on the radio. The super swore between crackles; they were already three men down. *Get out there and find him.* So, Dave had taken a car and gone back to Mount Tom Price. Casper's room was in the donger block, quiet in the day, al-foil in the windows against the sun. Dave had knocked for no answer. Knocked harder. And the door had popped off its catch.

Dave grabs fistfuls of hair, as if he can pull the memory out by the roots. Those black shapes in his mind are getting up now, the dead walking, toes dragging on the highway. Grit comes down from his scalp, trickles down his collar. The touch of it undoes his efforts; he can't help but see how Casper ended. Strewn, deflated and boneless, mouth and eyes choked with the black ore, blood still flowing from fingernails and ears, black where it touched the covers. The earth had eaten him. Then, one of those fingers had moved.

Oh. God.

Dave slaps at the grit under his collar. It runs down his back like tiny spiders. He wants to have a fit, rip his shirt off and scream his lungs out. But the grit catches in his waistband and the trickling stops.

He throws the nut wrench aside and spins out the jack. Two fingers throb, one on each hand. Sweat stings his eyes and makes icy tracks against his cheek. His breath blows white; the pink glow on the horizon grows. He kicks the jack over under the car; no time to repack it. He bolts for the driver's seat.

The breeze whips and yanks the door wide on its hinges. Dave yelps, straining to pull it closed. He turns the key instead. The wind whines. He hears it even as the engine turns over, then he grabs the door and slams it shut.

He jams into first and floors it. The tires bite the shoulder gravel and the Prado lurches onto bitumen.

The impact surprises him. Dave catches a blur of white before the Prado snaps sideways. His head collects the door window with a wet smack and the world spins over. He leans against the door and finds it open. Tumbles onto the road. Walks a few paces, then falls by the bull bar. Upside down, he sees a ute pointing into the gutter forty meters up the road, left bumper caved in, engine ticking. *Fuck*, he'd forgotten to check the mirror. Collected a car coming past, probably the one he'd heard before, perfect rotten timing.

In the Prado's headlights, the ute door opens and a man comes trotting over.

"Christ, mate, you ok?" he says, leaning down.

Dave hears himself groan. He puts his hands up to find the damage, feeling grit through warm blood.

"Jeez, Dave? Is that you?"

The voice is familiar. Craig, another bloke from the mine. Big hands pull him up, urgent. There's a rushing sound in Dave's ears. The ute turns right way up. Craig drags Dave towards it, insisting *they have to get out of here.* And maybe they can make it.

Then the road shoulder cracks, splitting like a lightning-struck tree, and from the rent comes a shape, half-man, half-earth, shedding soil from suggested arms and shoulders.

In the headlights, its red-dust skin splits like a sun-dried lake pan, the substrate black and oily. His eyes are Casper's, but the rest isn't a man at all. Earth come alive, and hungry.

Craig drops Dave and tries to run for it, but the thing is faster. One moment, Craig is on his feet, crab-stepping, and the next he is swallowed, leaving only a lingering cry. The ore thing remodels; in its bulk, a suggestion of a face, an eye socket, a row of teeth, shifting, reversing and nothing more.

Dave's head spins and he crashes to his knees. He wants to run, but he doesn't know which way is up. And then he realizes he is moving.

The thing has his foot. It drags him from the road, down into the scrub. The silvergrass scratches his back and his boots fill with stones. He struggles, but the hand on his boot crumbles down his pant leg. The grains burrow into his skin, and black ore comes tumbling down his chest, drawn on his breath. Sunlight won't save him, Dave knows this. Nothing will save him now.

He is filled before he can scream.

More from Charlie Nash

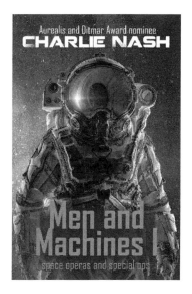

Four original science fiction stories, including the award shortlisted "Dellinger". Available in print and digital.

Four original stories of cyberpunk, steampunk and post-apocalyptic inspired fiction, including the award shortlisted "Alchemy & Ice". Available in print and digital.

Printed in Great Britain
by Amazon

85763195R00043